DATE DUE 1/04

AR LEVEL: 0.5

AR POINTS: 0.5

# Funny Faces

A very first picture book

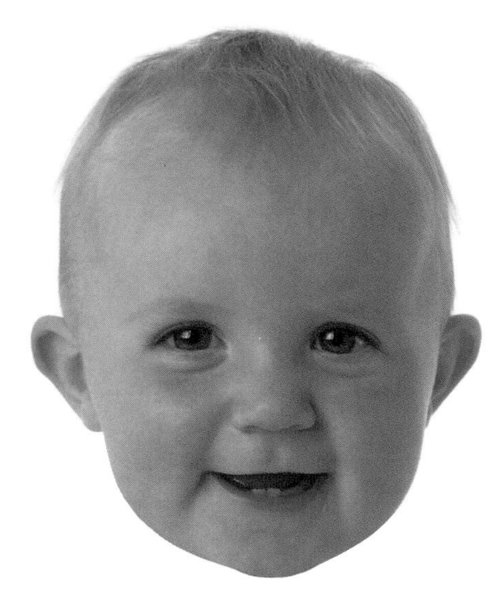

*The original publishers would like to thank the following children (and their parents) for appearing in this book: Rosie Anness, Karl Bolger, Andrew Brown, April Cain, Jordan Cleghorn-Woods, Emerald Coulthard, Alice Crawley, Arlena Dixon, Rianna Dixon, Safari George, Saffron George, Thomas Grant, Jasmine Haynes, Joseph Haynes, Erin Hoel, Alice Jenkins, Hannah Lie, Magdalena Nawrocka-Weekes, Conor Paul, Benjamin Phillips, Eloise Shepherd, Ella Wilks-Harper.*

**For a free color catalog describing Gareth Stevens Publishing's list of high-quality books and multimedia programs, call 1-800-542-2595 (USA) or 1-800-461-9120 (Canada). Gareth Stevens Publishing's Fax: (414) 225-0377.**

Library of Congress Cataloging-in-Publication Data

Funny faces: a very first picture book / consultant, Nicola Tuxworth.
p. cm. — (Pictures and words)
Includes bibliographical references and index.
Summary: Photographs and simple text show how babies' faces can reveal their feelings and moods.
ISBN 0-8368-2272-2 (lib. bdg.)
[1. Faces—Fiction. 2. Babies—Fiction.] I. Title. II. Series.
PZ7.F96625 1999
[E]—dc21 98-47412

This North American edition first published in 1999 by
**Gareth Stevens Publishing**
1555 North RiverCenter Drive, Suite 201
Milwaukee, WI 53212 USA



Senior editor: Caroline Beattie
Special photography: Lucy Tizard
Design and typesetting: Michael Leaman Design Partnership



Printed in Mexico

1 2 3 4 5 6 7 8 9 03 02 01 00 99

# Funny Faces

## A very first picture book

Nicola Tuxworth

Gareth Stevens Publishing
MILWAUKEE

I can't stop smiling today.

Mmmm, I'll just think about that for a while ...

Look at all the funny faces I can make!

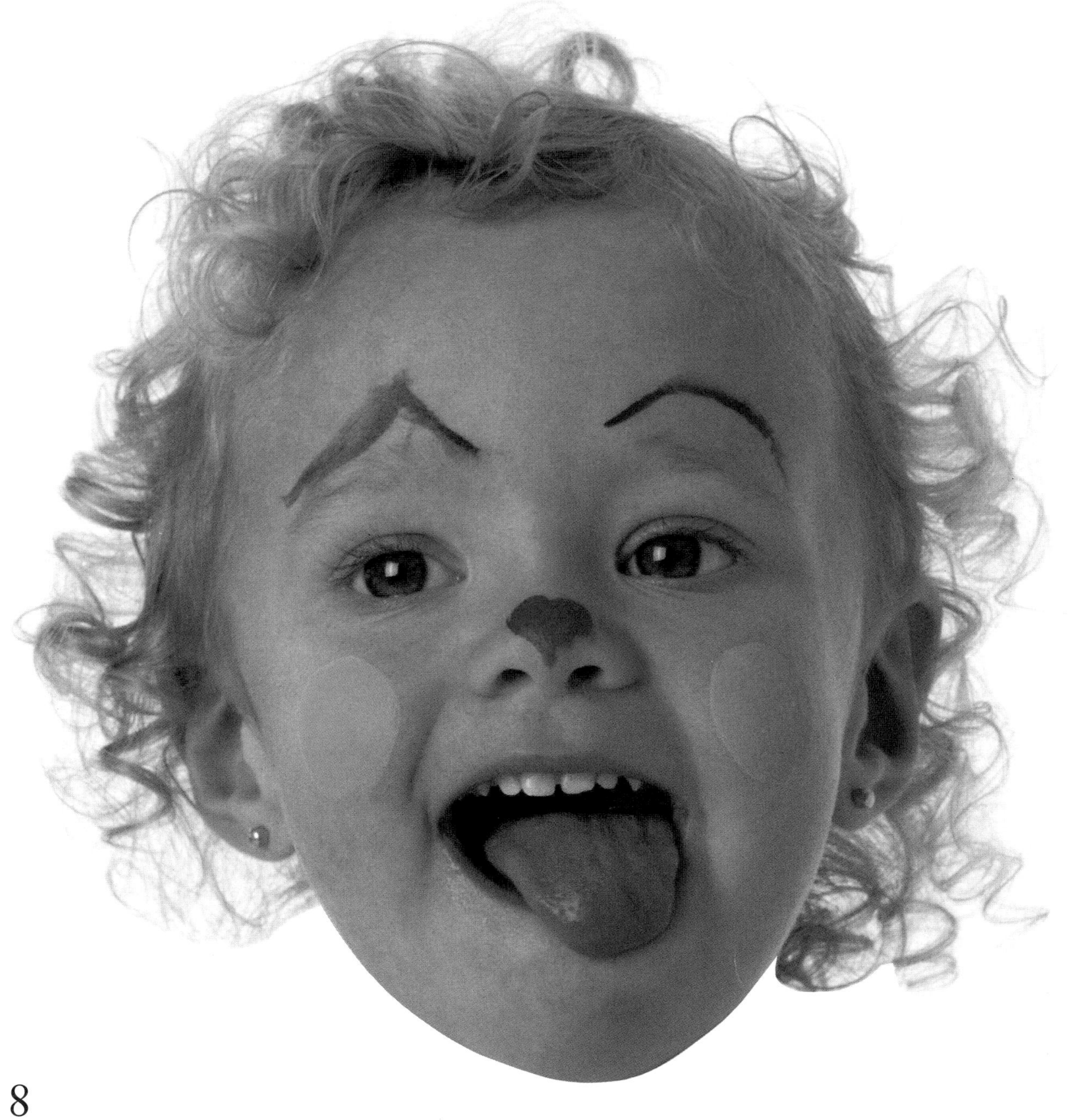

Do you like
my new hat?

Oh, what a terrible time I'm having.

Hello!
I'm a clown
today.

Look at me!
Peek-a-boo!

Go away!
I'm angry.

I'm just
a kittycat,
really.

Let's put on a show!

## Questions for Discussion

**1.** Point out your favorite "funny face" in this book. Why do you like it best? Try to make it yourself.

**2.** Find the pictures of the faces that look angry. How does a cat or dog show that it is angry? Can you think of ways that other animals show they are angry?

**3.** Find the pictures of the babies that are having a "terrible time." Why do you think they are crying?

**4.** Point out the pictures of the happy faces. What makes you feel happy?

**5.** When do you make funny faces? Why?

## More Books to Read


*Animal Faces.* Akira Satoh and Kyoko Toda (Kane Miller Book Publishing)

*Exploring Emotions (series).* Althea Braithwaite (Gareth Stevens)

*Fabulous Faces.* Shaila Awan, Editor (Dorling Kindersley)

*Face Painting.* Margaret Lincoln (Copper Beech)

*Five-Minute Faces.* (Random House)

*Making Masks and Crazy Faces.* Jen Green (Gloucester Press)

*Super Masks and Fun Face Painting.* Teddy Cameron Long (Sterling Publishing)

*Wow! Babies!* Penny Gentieu (Crown Publishing)

## Videos

*Clown Face.* (Pyramid Film & Video)

*Faces and Feelings.* (Agency for Instructional Technology)

*Feelings.* (Churchill Media)

*How to Go From Mad to Glad.* (Sunburst Communications)

## Web Sites

www.EnchantedLearning.com/crafts/

www.ctw.org/

Some web sites stay current longer than others. For further web sites, use your search engines to locate the following topics: *anger, clowns, face painting, happiness, joy,* and *sadness.*

## Glossary-Index

**angry:** not happy about something; feeling mad and upset. (p. 19)

**clown:** a person who dresses in a costume and does tricks or who acts in a funny way to make people laugh. (p. 14)

**hat:** a covering worn on the head, such as a cap or bonnet. (p. 10)

**peek-a-boo:** a game where you hide your face, then peek out suddenly and say "peek-a-boo." (p. 16)

**terrible:** very, very bad; horrible. (p. 12)

**think:** to take time to run things through your mind. (p. 6)

**while:** an amount of time. (p. 6)